Silly Fred

by Karen Wagner

illustrated by Normand Chartier

Macmillan Publishing Company
New York

For *Emmy*—K.W.

For Molly and Sam's Cousin,
Boobly Taylor G.—N.C.

Macmillan Publishing Company, 866 Third Avenue, New York, NY 10022
Collier Macmillan Canada, Inc.

Printed and bound in Singapore First American Edition 10 9 8 7 6 5 4 3 2 1

The text of this book is set in 16 point ITC Zapf International Light.
The illustrations are rendered in pencil and watercolor.

Library of Congress Cataloging-in-Publication Data
Wagner, Karen. Silly Fred/by Karen Wagner; illustrated by Normand Chartier.—1st American ed.
*   p.   cm. Summary: Silly Fred Pig decides to be more serious, like a beaver, only to*
discover that life is not much fun without somersaults and song.
ISBN 0-02-792280-4
[1. Pigs—Fiction.]   I. Chartier, Normand, date, ill.   II. Title.
PZ7.W12428Si 1989   [E]—dc19   88-22620 CIP AC

Fred was a silly pig. He was so silly his
mother often said, "Fred, you are a silly pig.
I wonder what makes you that way."

Fred thought it was because he liked to sing.
"Beedly beedly bee, boodly boodly boo, boo-hoo,
boo-hoo, boo, boo, boo."

Fred's father thought it was because Fred
turned somersaults before bed—from one end
of the bed to the other and back again.

The first night his father saw Fred somersault, he walked quietly into the living room and said, "Fred is upstairs turning somersaults on his bed."

Fred's mother said, "He is such a silly pig.
I wonder what makes him that way."

Fred did not mind being silly. He didn't
know any other way to be.

One day Fred was walking in the woods collecting leaves for a leaf necklace. He sang. "Leafity leafity leaf, loofity loofity loo, loo-hoo, loo-hoo, loo, loo, loo." He was trying to choose between an orange and a yellow leaf when he saw a beaver sitting on a log.

"What color leaf should I choose?" Fred asked the beaver.

"Who cares?" said the beaver.

Fred thought the beaver was being silly. "That's right. Who cares?" said Fred, and threw the leaves in the air. An orange leaf landed on the beaver's nose.

The beaver pulled it off. "I've seen you before," he said. "I've heard you singing silly songs. I do not like them. I do not like you."

Fred felt sad. No one had ever said they did not like him.

The beaver looked into Fred's eyes. "I have also heard that you are fond of turning somersaults on your bed. That is the silliest thing I have ever heard."

Fred sat down. He did not want to make a
leaf necklace. He did not want to sing. He did
not want to turn somersaults.

He sat and thought. Never had he felt so sad.

When he finally looked up, the beaver was
gone. The sky was turning dark. Fred slowly,
without singing, walked home.

He opened the door and said to his mother, "I have been a silly pig. I will not be silly anymore."

Fred's mother thought this was a silly new game and said, "That's a good idea, Fred."

Fred went to bed without singing or turning somersaults.

When Fred was asleep, Fred's father said,
"What's wrong with Fred? He didn't turn any
somersaults tonight."

His mother said, "Now that I think about it,
I haven't heard him sing a silly song all day."

The next morning Fred's parents took him to the doctor. Fred's father said, "Doctor, Fred didn't turn a single somersault last night."

Fred's mother said, "He didn't sing one silly song."

The doctor looked in Fred's eyes, ears, and throat. He took his temperature. He looked at Fred from his head to his toes.

"I'm sorry," he said. "There's nothing I can do."

Weeks later, Fred was walking through the woods when he came upon a small house. He peeked in the window. Inside was the beaver he had met long ago. The beaver was washing dishes. Fred watched as the beaver washed one dish, then the next, and the next.

He watched as the beaver read a book,

dusted the furniture,

and cooked dinner.

All the while the beaver did not do one silly thing. Even though it was getting dark, Fred stayed to watch. When it was time for bed, the beaver pulled down the covers, climbed into bed, and went to sleep.

Suddenly, Fred smiled a small smile.

As he walked home, the smile got bigger and
bigger and bigger, until it was the same smile
Fred used to smile before he met the beaver.

"That beaver is not silly," he said to a tree. "That beaver is not silly at all. Why, he doesn't even turn somersaults. He just goes to sleep."

"I don't want to be like that beaver," Fred said to a rock. "I'll bet he doesn't even know how to sing."

By the time Fred got home he was singing.
"Happily happily hay, hoopily hoopily hoo, hoo,
hoo, hoo."

When he opened the door his mother and father hugged him. "Fred," his mother said, "you're back."

"And you're singing," his father said. "And I do believe it's a silly song."

That night Fred turned five extra
somersaults before bed.

Fred was a silly pig again.